Z the Zebra
Goes to Kindergarten

LYNETTE KOCH

LifeRich Publishing is a registered trademark of The Reader's Digest Association, Inc.

LifeRich Publishing books may be ordered through booksellers or by contacting:

LifeRich Publishing
1663 Liberty Drive
Bloomington, IN 47403
www.liferichpublishing.com
844-686-9607

Because of the dynamic nature of the Internet, any web addresses or links contained in this book may have changed since publication and may no longer be valid. The views expressed in this work are solely those of the author and do not necessarily reflect the views of the publisher, and the publisher hereby disclaims any responsibility for them.

Any people depicted in stock imagery provided by Getty Images are models, and such images are being used for illustrative purposes only. Certain stock imagery © Getty Images.

ISBN: 978-1-4897-3945-2 (sc)
978-1-4897-3946-9 (hc)
978-1-4897-3944-5 (e)

Print information available on the last page.

LifeRich Publishing rev. date: 11/22/2021

Z the Zebra
Goes to Kindergarten

Early one morning, in an African meadow of green,

Was a miraculous and amazing sight, like no one had ever seen.

A precious little guy was born that day; his parents named him Z.

He was a brilliant sight as he lay there sunning near a jackalberry tree.

A zebra with no stripes but full of spots in rainbow colors that were all a glow.

Such a beautiful sight to see! How did this happen? No one would probably ever know.

Years went by so quickly, and five years had flown by so fast—

Z had been busy helping others with his lighted spots, whenever they would ask.

He spent some time planting flower seeds; he loved to see them grow.

He watered and weeded them, and entered them in the big flower show.

He planted every size and color, placing them with care while on the ground he sat.

(He also grew these because his mother loved to wear flowers in her hat.)

He entered the flower contest one day at the summer fair.

His flower won the grand prize: it was a perfect yellow, so beautiful and rare.

The prize was a beanbag toss game shaped like a four-leaf clover.

It was a fun game to play with family and when his friends would gather and come over.

Soon it was time to plan a fifth birthday party, what kind of theme would be fun?

Maybe superheroes, race cars, soccer, outer space, rainbows, or an obstacle course outside in the sun.

Z loved everything about a rainbow. It reminded him of God's promises and how much he cares for each and every one.

God offers hope, peace, and love and wants us to have a wonderful life—the reason he sent us Jesus, his one and only son.

A birthday full of rainbow decorations, balloons, sprinkled cupcakes, presents, and pin the spots on the zebra game.

Z was so surprised at how many were at his party and ever so grateful for all the friends who came.

Next, he needed to plan for kindergarten. Soon it would be time to start school.

The thought of learning the alphabet, numbers, reading, and writing was kind of scary but could be extremely cool!

Z would need a backpack to hold his colors, scissors, folders, notebook, pencils, and glue.

A special day was planned with lunch and ice cream, then searching for school supplies. Z picked out a backpack that was his favorite color, blue.

His momma took him to get his eyes checked. He was having a little trouble seeing and was anxious what the doctor might say—

He had noticed some things he could not see clearly when he went about his day.

The eye doctor said Z needed glasses as he was farsighted. Z didn't really know what that meant.

But was told to pick out some glasses, what color do you think he picked? Yes, blue! They made him look smart, he was a handsome gent.

As the first day of kindergarten was approaching, his tummy felt like it was full of bubbles. His mother called them butterflies.

He didn't like this feeling at all and tried not to think about it because tears would fill his eyes.

Z wondered if his teacher would like him. Would he make friends? Would he get lost or be smart enough to learn?

All the others going to school probably felt this way, and they all had the same concern.

Z was used to hanging out with his family and friends and playing every day.

Not sure he would like this separation but maybe it would be fine, and he would probably be OK.

Mother said, "Z, do not be so anxious. Everything will truly be fine. Ask God to help you and to fill you with his peace.

He is always with you and keeps watch over you. His love and help for you will never end, and it will never cease."

Z was told just to be his sweet self, to be kind to everyone, and to never ever be mean or cruel.

"Sit quietly, be a good listener, and ask questions if you should need to—and follow the teacher's rule.

In no time at all, you will have your routine, and you will see that your school day is fun.

We are all here to help you, and always remember how much we love you, our precious little son."

16

He went to the school to look on the list to see in whose class he might be.

He started at the top with the letter A until he found, last but not least, his one-letter name, Z.

Z was excited as he looked at all the names typed on his class list.

His teacher's name was Miss Love. Could it get any better than this?

She must have been sent from heaven with a sweet name like that.

Someone told him that in her class she had a super cool, adorable, blue point Siamese cat.

To have a cat in the school was going to be fun; it was sure to be a big hit.

They would all take turns taking the cat home. Everyone had a chance to baby … or I should say, to cat sit.

In school they practiced their ABCs, counted, colored pictures, cut out shapes, played games, and so much more.

Being five was really great, even better than the days of being four.

Z's favorite part of the day was going out to recess to play with his friends. He would make his spots glow!

They liked to play Red Light, Green Light, and asked Z to light up his spots to let them know when to stay or when to go.

His teacher asked Z if he would like to help the students learn all about their colors.

They all thought this was so fun as Z's spots would light up. Z was always glad when he could be of help to others.

Sharing is Caring

Z's kindergarten classroom had students from different backgrounds and from all walks of life.

Miss Love's goal was to teach kindness, respect, and acceptance, and to keep her classroom free from all strife:

"Love one another and love your neighbor as yourself is what is on God's heart.

We can all do this together, if we try and each do our part."

One of Z's classmates did not have his own markers, colors, or glue.

Z was quick to offer to share his; he knew this was the right thing to do.

One day on the playground, Z saw some others picking on a student from his class who was very shy.

His spots of red got really bright as he went over to see if he could help—he knew at least he should try.

Sometimes Z's spots would all light up at once, and other times just one at a time.

You could usually tell what he was feeling—his spots were always a clear sign.

The students loved it when Z would tell them one of his many jokes—they thought he was very funny—

Like "Why are fish so smart? Because they live in schools, or "Why did the bee get married? Because she found her honey!"

Or "Why did the student eat his homework? Because the teacher told him it was piece of cake."

Sometimes he would make them laugh so hard that their little bellies would ache.

Z ended up having lots of friends and a successful kindergarten year.

He was looking forward to summer break and then first grade; he now knew he had nothing at all to fear.

Kindergarten turned out to be even greater than Z had ever dreamed.

He loved his teacher, friends, and school. He was so happy, even more than before his spots were radiant and all agleam.

A new command I give you: Love one another. As I have loved you, so you must love one another. (John 13:34)

I am putting a rainbow in the clouds. It is a sign of agreement between me and the earth. When I bring clouds over the earth a rainbow appears in the clouds. Then I will remember my agreement. It is between me and you and every living thing. Floodwaters will never again destroy all life on earth. Genesis 9:13-15

CPSIA information can be obtained
at www.ICGtesting.com
Printed in the USA
BVHW021341131221
623921BV00008B/90